Schnitzel

A Cautionary Tale for Lazy Louts

Stephanie Shaw ~ Illustrated by Kevin M. Barry

PUBLISHED BY SLEEPING BEAR PRESS

I am Apprentice Schnitzel.
I once served Sir Willibald.
His wizardry was world-renowned
And I was quite enthralled.

But Willibald was very strict.
His rules were etched in stone.
My duty was to clean the house
And leave the spells alone.

No shortcuts to be taken.
No task too large to shirk.
But I was quite a lazy lout
And did not like to work.

Before I went to bed one night
I read chores from my list:
Be sure to vacuum every room;
No corner should be missed.

Of all the housework left to me
This one I liked the least.
Our temperamental vacuum
Behaved like such a beast.

The doorbell chimed at midnight.
Startled, I awoke.
A stranger stood upon the porch
Draped in an opera cloak.

Goooood evening, oozed the salesman.
His face was ghostly pale.
If you have a vacuum problem,
I have just the thing for sale!

Allow me in to demonstrate.
I'll finish in no time.
I'll do your work. You'll rest in peace.
And I'll not charge a dime.

No charge to do the work for me!
What harm to ask him in?
Step right inside, I told him.
He gave a toothy grin.

With a flourish he unveiled The Thing
And plugged it in a socket.
The motor roared and flames shot out;
It took off like a rocket.

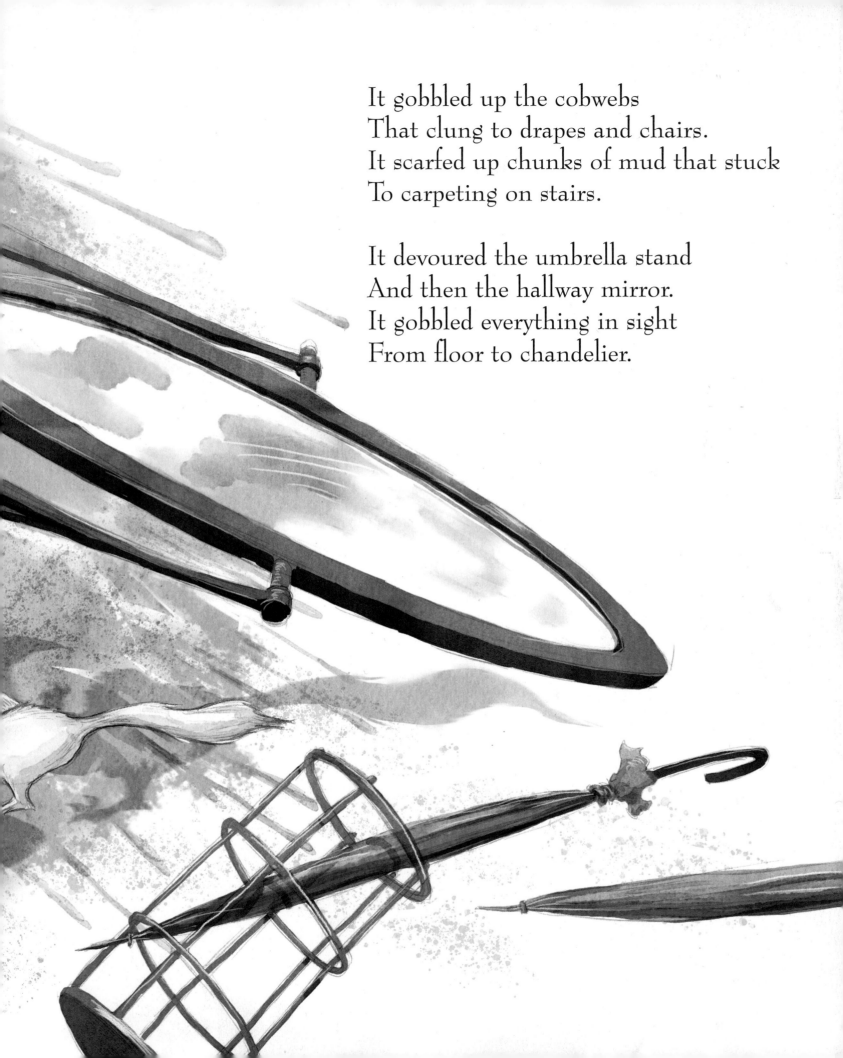

It gobbled up the cobwebs
That clung to drapes and chairs.
It scarfed up chunks of mud that stuck
To carpeting on stairs.

It devoured the umbrella stand
And then the hallway mirror.
It gobbled everything in sight
From floor to chandelier.

I watched in horror as he worked,
The vacuum cleaner slurping,
Consuming tables, rugs, and lamps—
Exhaling sounds like burping.

It swallowed all the dishes
From the cupboards and the sink.
It even ate the garbage
Leaving nothing but the stink.

There was little left to vacuum
Once this inhaling broom
Consumed the household contents
And the air out of the room.

But finally The Thing was full.
It belched, *I beg your pardon*.
Digesting the entire house
And leaving just the garden.

It seems my work is done here,
I heard the salesman say.
But perhaps I'll have a little bite
And then be on my way.

What possibly could save me
From this ghastly twist of fate?
I wished I'd done the work myself
But now it was too late.

I found myself back in my room.
The house was as before.
And a scowling Wizard Willibald
Was standing at the door.

Amid the dust and grime and mud
The garlic fumes were thick.
He handed me a mop and pail:
You'll find these do the trick!

Since then 'til now I do my work
And all that it requires.
Nevermore to ask for help
From door-to-door vampires.

Some Wizardly Writing of Your Own

This is a story that you can magically change into one of your very own.

Schnitzel is a "retelling" of a poem titled "Der Zauberlehrling" ("The Sorcerer's Apprentice") that was written in 1797 by the German poet Johann Wolfgang von Goethe. In that poem, a lazy apprentice uses his master's spell to fetch water. The spell spirals out of control with water reaching a flood stage before the sorcerer appears to stop it. And *that* story was a retelling of a poem written by a Greek writer named Lucian in AD 150!

In 1897 the composer Paul Dukas retold the story in a beautiful symphony. There is another more modern version in which the apprentice is a young girl and it is a sewing machine that gets out of control! The story has been around for a long, long time. And it has been told and retold in books, movies, and in many different ways.

You can write a retelling of "The Sorcerer's Apprentice," too. In a retelling there is enough of the story that stays the same that we can recognize the original. There are enough *changes* to make it different.

First, read a traditional telling of "The Sorcerer's Apprentice." If you were retelling the story your own way, how would you make it different? What would stay the same?

Could the sorcerer be a master baker with a helper and an out-of-control cupcake machine?

How could this story be told if it was at a zoo?
A ranch? A sea aquarium?

What would happen if the sorcerer was in trouble instead of the apprentice?

Would you tell your story in rhyme or in prose?
In music? In pictures?

It's up to you!

—Stephanie Shaw